Wild Things

Animals of the Jungle

By Czeena Devera

Elephants live in the jungle.

Gorillas live in the jungle.

Monkeys live in the jungle.

Jaguars live in the jungle.

Lemurs live in the jungle.

Frogs live in the jungle.

Koalas live in the jungle.

Tigers live in the jungle.

Snakes live in the jungle.

Parrots live in the jungle.

Sloths live in the jungle.

Lizards live in the jungle.

Word List

sight words

elephants
jungle
gorillas
monkeys
jaguars
lemurs
frogs
koalas
tigers
snakes
parrots
sloths
lizards

60 Words

Elephants live in the jungle.
Gorillas live in the jungle.
Monkeys live in the jungle.
Jaguars live in the jungle.
Lemurs live in the jungle.
Frogs live in the jungle.
Koalas live in the jungle.
Tigers live in the jungle.
Snakes live in the jungle.
Parrots live in the jungle.
Sloths live in the jungle.
Lizards live in the jungle.

Published in the United States of America by Cherry Lake Publishing
Ann Arbor, Michigan
www.cherrylakepublishing.com

Photo Credits: ©Dirk Ercken/Shutterstock.com, front cover, back cover,15; ©ehtesham/Shutterstock.com, 1; ©Benz Sorasak/Shutterstock.com, 2; ©Simon Eeman/Shutterstock.com, 3; ©Nick Fox/Shutterstock.com, 4; ©Kris Wiktor/Shutterstock.com, 5; ©Ryan M. Bolton/Shutterstock.com, 6; ©Kurit afshen/Shutterstock.com, 7; ©worldswildlifewonders/Shutterstock.com, 8; ©Michal Ninger/Shutterstock.com, 9; ©Attila JANDI/Shutterstock.com, 10; ©Jiri Hrebicek/Shutterstock.com, 11; ©Damsea/Shutterstock.com, 12; ©SARIN KUNTHONG/Shutterstock.com, 13

Cherry Blossom Press is an imprint of Cherry Lake Publishing.

Library of Congress Cataloging-in-Publication Data

Names: Devera, Czeena, author.
Title: Animals of the jungle / by Czeena Devera.
Description: Ann Arbor : Cherry Lake Publishing, [2019] | Series: Wild things | Audience: Pre-school, excluding K.
Identifiers: LCCN 20[illegible]50| ISBN 9781534149816 (paperback) | ISBN 9781534148383 (pdf) | ISBN 9781534151246 (hosted ebook)
Subjects: LCSH: Jungle animals–Juvenile literature.
Classification: LCC QL112 .D48 2019 | DDC 591.73–dc23
LC record available at https://lccn.loc.gov/2019006050

Printed in the United States of America
Corporate Graphics

CHERRY BLOSSOM PRESS